READY, SET, JUMP!

Diane Bair and Pamela Wright

Contents

Rigby

READY, SET, JUMP!

Imagine stepping out of a plane thousands of feet in the air and . . . falling . . . falling . . . falling . . . until your parachute opens. Now you drift like a bird, floating gently down to Earth.

If this sounds exciting, then the sport of skydiving is for you! Many people learn to skydive each year. Some jump for fun. Others join teams and enter skydiving contests.

Do you want to get an idea of what skydiving is like? There are three ways of getting started. Take a look at the pictures. Which one do you like?

You don't have to decide now. Just come along and get the feel of the air!

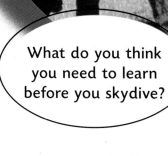

What do you think you need to learn before you skydive?

ONE KIND OF JUMP

Before you go skydiving, you have to decide what kind of jump you want to take. There are three main ways to begin skydiving. Choose the one you like the most. You also have to think about the drop zone, the skydiving spot you go to.

With one kind of jump, you can jump out of the plane by yourself the very first time you go up. First, though, you have to train for about four or five hours on the ground. Then you go up about 3,000 feet off the ground in a small plane.

But don't worry. You're not on your own. A line fastened to the plane is pulled to open your **parachute.** You'll have about two or three seconds of **free fall** before the parachute opens.

Later, as you do more jumps and get more training, you'll learn to pull the **ripcord** yourself.

How safe is skydiving?

One skydiving instructor says that thanks to improvements in gear and safety guidelines, skydivers do not often get hurt. He says that jumping out of a plane is safer than driving in busy traffic.

What would you tell a friend about why skydiving is safe?

THE FREE FALL JUMP

The free fall is a quicker way of getting the real feel of skydiving. You jump out of the plane at 10,000–12,000 feet above the ground with two jump masters holding on to you. They guide you during a 50-second free fall, until you pull the ripcord to open your parachute.

The free fall jump requires about five hours of training before your first jump.

Why do you think people would jump from a plane at 10,000 feet?

What if the parachute doesn't open?

All skydivers have a main parachute and a backup parachute. There are laws about who can pack parachutes and how often they must be checked. Safety features include a device that works by itself and pulls the ripcord if the skydiver can't.

THE TANDEM JUMP

The quickest way of getting in and out of a plane is the **tandem** jump. In this kind of jump, you simply "take a ride" with a jump master. Both you and the jump master wear **harnesses.** But only the jump master wears the parachute.

In a tandem jump, your harness is fastened to the front of the jump master's harness. You jump together and free fall together for about 30 seconds. Then, you both land under one very big parachute.

Getting ready for the tandem jump is a lot easier than the other two ways. You need only about 15–45 minutes of ground training!

In the United States, safety guidelines are set by the people who make skydiving gear. Some people think that tandem jumping is unsafe.

Why do you think some people might not think this method is safe?

YOUR JUMP

You've decided that you'll feel safe taking a tandem jump. Safer, actually, because you'll be fastened to a jump master. Also, you think tandem jumping makes sense because it takes the least time to prepare for.

Almost before you know it, your plane is high in the sky. Your harness is already attached to the front of the jump master's harness.

You and the jump master kneel beside the plane's door. "Are you ready?" he asks.

The door opens, and you feel a rush of cold air. You move to the edge of the open door and look down at puffy clouds and blue sky.

"Ready! Set! Jump!"

Do you think people ever decide at the last minute not to jump? Why or why not?

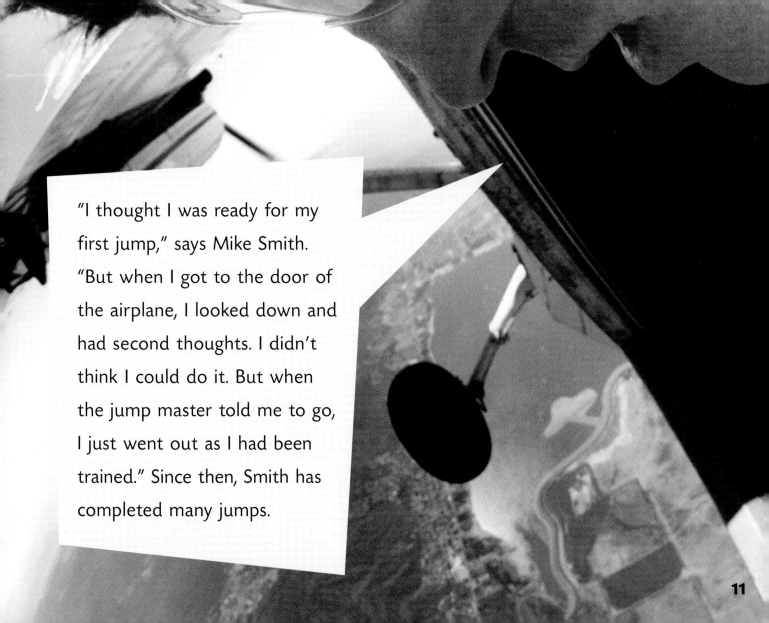

"I thought I was ready for my first jump," says Mike Smith. "But when I got to the door of the airplane, I looked down and had second thoughts. I didn't think I could do it. But when the jump master told me to go, I just went out as I had been trained." Since then, Smith has completed many jumps.

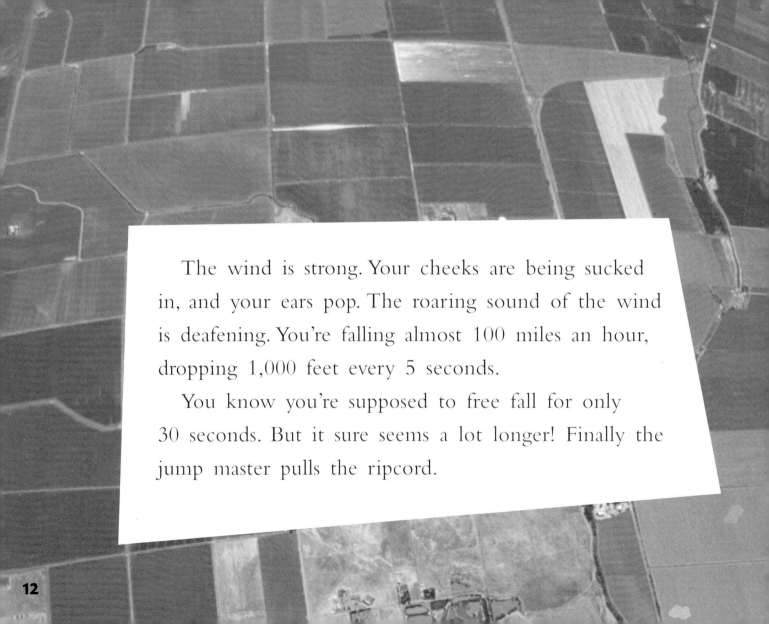

The wind is strong. Your cheeks are being sucked in, and your ears pop. The roaring sound of the wind is deafening. You're falling almost 100 miles an hour, dropping 1,000 feet every 5 seconds.

You know you're supposed to free fall for only 30 seconds. But it sure seems a lot longer! Finally the jump master pulls the ripcord.

Whoosh! The parachute opens with a jerk. The loud roar of the wind stops. You hear the flapping of the top of the parachute above you.

You are floating in air. The land below looks like a patchwork quilt. Streets and roads are like ink scribbles on paper. The houses and trees look like toys.

How do you think you would feel when the parachute opened?

YOUR LANDING

By pulling the parachute's left and right cords at the same time, the jump master guides the parachute and slows it down.

The ground is getting closer and closer. You can now see the marks on the landing field, and the jump master aims for them. Falling . . . falling . . . falling . . .

How would a jump master help you?

Plop! You drop softly, feet first, on the ground. What a thrill!

Would you like to learn to skydive? There's just one catch. Students usually must be at least 18 years old.

In the meantime, you can learn all about skydiving by reading and watching videos about this exciting sport. You can also ask an adult to take you to a drop zone, where you can watch skydivers. And you can start saving your money!

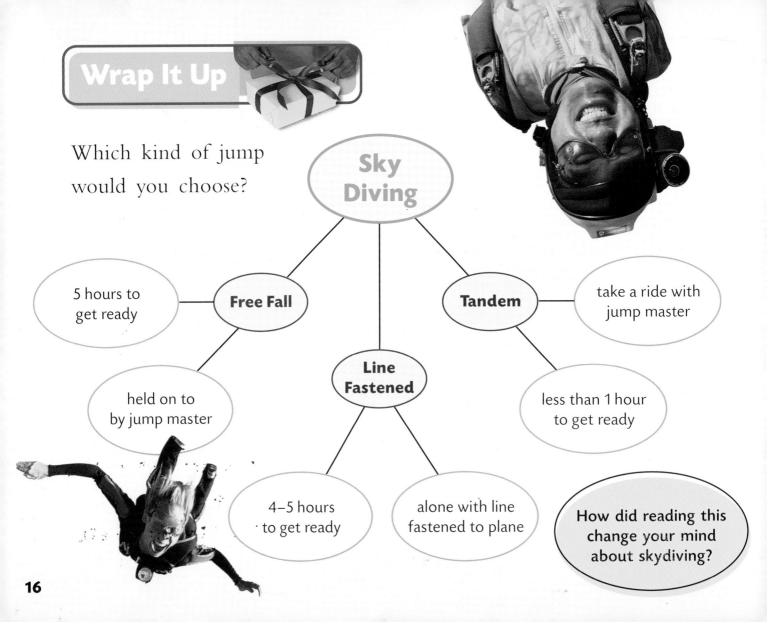

Wrap It Up

Which kind of jump would you choose?

Sky Diving

Free Fall
- 5 hours to get ready
- held on to by jump master

Line Fastened
- 4–5 hours to get ready
- alone with line fastened to plane

Tandem
- take a ride with jump master
- less than 1 hour to get ready

How did reading this change your mind about skydiving?